ALSO BY THE A

The Nihilist: A Novel

Beauty in Decay:
Photos from Chernobyl

I HATE TRAVELING

A TRAVELOGUE

KEIJO KANGUR

I Hate Traveling
A Travelogue

First Edition

Copyright © 2021 Keijo Kangur

This is a work of nonfiction. All of the characters, places and incidents are based on real life. Some names have been changed.

Photos by Maria Sütt
& Keijo Kangur

Vector art by Maria Sütt

Book design by Keijo Kangur

ISBN: 979-8-7390-7217-7

www.keijokangur.com

That which interests most people leaves me without any interest at all. This includes a list of things such as: social dancing, riding roller coasters, going to zoos, picnics, movies, planetariums, watching tv, baseball games; going to funerals, weddings, parties, basketball games, auto races, poetry readings, museums, rallies, demonstrations, protests, children's plays, adult plays . . . I am not interested in beaches, swimming, skiing, Christmas, New Year's, the 4th of July, rock music, world history, space exploration, pet dogs, soccer, cathedrals and great works of Art. How can a man who is interested in almost nothing write about anything? Well, I do.

—Charles Bukowski,
Shakespeare Never Did This

Triglav   Bled

Ljubljana

Postojna

DAY ONE
MONDAY

TRAVELING MUST BE one of the most overrated things in the world. Right next to children, marriage, traditions, religion, sports, Hollywood actors, humanity, life, atoms, and the universe.

Why? Because it's too expensive. It takes too long to get there. It's too inconvenient. And when you're finally there you discover that there are endless lines everywhere you go—something that was clearly missing from the pretty brochures. Moreover, most of the destinations have been so over-romanticized and overhyped over time that they couldn't possibly match reality anymore.

Not to mention the fact that everything's just so goddamn commercialized, having long been turned into a mere product to be sold and consumed by the masses. Meaning wherever you go there are always endless lines of people consuming the same fucking product that you are, constantly reminding you that your experience is neither unique nor special. And if there are too many people attracted to something, it's usually for the same reason as why flies are attracted to shit.

However, since I hadn't had a proper vacation for a while now and was burned out from work, I felt I needed one. A colleague from the office, who had long black hair and listened to heavy metal, had one day randomly recommended Slovenia to me. The only thing I knew about Slovenia at the time was that the US president's stupid fucking wife was from there, which was not exactly an endorsement.

Yet when I looked up Slovenia online, I saw that it also had beautiful mountains, vibrant green valleys, and ancient castles, which was enough for me and Morrigan to buy the plane tickets.

OUR FIRST FLIGHT went from Tallinn to Helsinki, where we took a connecting flight to Slovenia, which is nestled between Italy, Austria, and Croatia. Helsinki, by the way, is above Tallinn. Slovenia, on the other hand, is below Tallinn. Thus, to get to Slovenia from Tallinn, the plane first takes you *further* away from it. Somehow, somebody thought this makes sense.

On the flight to Helsinki, we had these rotten seats where the two passengers in front of us were facing towards us, eyeing our every move, or so it had seemed.

Also, a new experience for me on this particular flight was that I had to learn some additional safety instructions because I was sitting right next to the emergency exit. Well fuck that, I thought, as the stewardess handed me a manual regarding my extra responsibilities. How the shit was this my job?

Besides, if the plane was *already* going down, I would hope that it went down fast and hard and that there would be no survivors. Cause that's just the kind of guy I am.

HELSINKI AIRPORT WAS a fucking nightmare. There were so many people everywhere that you could hardly move. At least the part we were in. For you see, when Morrigan and I went on an intercontinental flight to China the year before from the very same airport, it was actually quite pleasant. Why? Because intercontinental flights have a much larger and nicer section for travelers than do flights inside Europe.

Morrigan suggested that this was so because you could milk more money out of the people on the intercontinental flights since they were already paying much more and tended to be wealthier. She was probably right. Airports, after all, are known for the psychological tricks they pull on you in order to make you spend more—for instance, forcing you to walk through a store to get to your plane, which makes zero fucking sense.

Anyway, the airport was overcrowded, overloud, overpriced, and the food was godawful, as I soon learned after buying one of the shittiest and most expensive sandwiches that I had ever eaten. The beer I washed it down with had also cost me a small fortune. And don't even get me started on the fancy restaurant where we didn't go to because their prices were just fucking insane.

But the main problem I had with the airport wasn't the prices. It was the people. There were too many of them. And it goes without saying that the more people there are at any given place, the worse that place becomes on all accounts. There is no man who can be by himself alone so contemptible as a body of men, as Chamfort said, and there is no body of men that can be so contemptible as the public at large.

And it's not only airports but also beaches, shops, cinemas, clubs, tourist attractions, zoos, restaurants, bars, concerts, festivals, museums and gangbangs that suffer from the exact same problem—that there are just too many fucking people everywhere you go, and they often bring their stupid fucking children with them. Well . . . maybe not to the gangbangs, but still.

And flying in an airplane, you get to be cramped up with the fuckers in a small space for hours on end! Though you were flying through heaven, it often felt like you were in hell.

WHEN WE GOT on the flight to Slovenia, which was to take two and a half hours, I discovered that there was neither any in-flight entertainment onboard nor any free food or alcohol. At first, this realization had made me rather miserable. Until I discovered that I could get free alcohol with the frequent flyer miles I had accrued from the year before, which cheered me the fuck up.

I bought some beer and red wine and began drinking both whilst reading a collection of Bukowski's short stories called South of No North. There were some pretty good ones in there; for instance, the one where a guy buys a mannequin and tries to fuck it. At the same time, Morrigan was reading the most cheerful book ever written—The Conspiracy Against the Human Race. It's so cheerful, in fact, that after I read it, I was depressed for two months straight.

Aside from reading and drinking, there was one more activity I enjoyed doing in airplanes, which was farting. And so I tried to let out as many of them as I could—big fat fellows, long windy ones, quick little merry cracks and a lot of tiny little naughty farties ending in a long gush, as James Joyce so poetically put it. For some reason, I took great delight in forcing my stink upon perfect strangers, my fetid molecules traveling up their nostrils, briefly invading their consciousness.

WHEN WE TOUCHED down in Slovenia, I saw that there were mountains in every direction that I looked. This immediately made me feel good. Mountains had always made me feel good. Perhaps it had something to do with living in a flat country. Perhaps the same applied to living with a flat girlfriend.

Morrigan had scheduled a taxi to pick us up from the airport, so we began searching for it. It took us a while, but eventually we managed to locate it in the parking lot. And then we were on our way to the town called Bled.

"How was your flight?" asked the blonde woman who was driving the taxi.

"Not too bad," Morrigan answered. "At least there weren't any crying children."

To this the driver responded that she, on the other hand, liked having as many children as possible on a flight because she was afraid of flying and thought that if there were lots of children on the airplane then God would think twice before "taking them."

My God, I thought, listening to her lunacy. Why were religious people always such fucking nutcases?

IT TOOK US about half an hour to arrive at the hotel. Unfortunately, since we had waited until the last minute with booking it, it was a few kilometers away from town and it was far from luxurious.

Thus, after settling into the hotel, which was ran

by a Chinese family and had a surprisingly decent view of a nearby mountain, we began walking towards the town of Bled.

It was hot as hell and it was a long walk. Also, since there were no sidewalks, we had to walk on the side of the road, cars racing by us. This annoyed me since I was used to walking on sidewalks like a civilized person. After having to suffer this shit after the long and unpleasant flights, I was beginning to get pissed off.

When we finally arrived in Bled, we went to the nearest supermarket to buy some beer. *A lot* of beer. For I often had the fear of not having a beer nearby when I needed one, which meant that I liked to keep plenty stocked.

What I found interesting in the supermarket was that some of the beer cans on the shelf were upside down, even though their labels were the correct way up. I soon figured out why—since the beer was unfiltered, when you turned it around, the muck sank from the top to the bottom, which was rather clever.

After we had finished loading my backpack full of beer, we started searching for a restaurant where to have dinner. As we walked through the streets of Bled, we constantly saw—or rather *heard*—British tourists everywhere. Much to my dismay, it seemed that this was one of their holiday destinations.

How did one recognize a British tourist? Well,

there was usually the fat balding dad with anger issues, who thinks he's awfully clever when in fact he's not. Along with his ugly old cow of a wife with a prolapsed uterus from giving birth too much. As well as their three stupid children who are either all on drugs or soon will be.

And then of course there were the *chavellers* who you could tell from a mile away by their ugly fucking slang: Oi, I'm knackered! That's brilliant, innit? Lovely, yeah? Bloody hell, I'm pissed! I'm chuffed to bits! Fancy a fag, mate? Bollocks! Is he taking the piss? Wanker! Bugger! Rubbish! Blimey! Blooming! Blighter! Pish. Posh. Fuck. Off. Sometimes I wish I was born deaf.

And that . . . *accent*, man. You know, that smug and self-assured way of speaking, even though they sound like fucking peasants. As the saying goes, the stronger the accent, the stupider the person. Or at least it should.

But enough about that. Eventually, we found a pub that looked all right and didn't seem too pretentious. Not that any of the eating places in Bled did since it seemed that most of them only served pizza or paninis. And the places that served paninis all had the exact same identical stock image of the same fucking panini, which clearly did not match reality.

Anyway, we sat down on the terrace, which had a decent view of the nearby Lake Bled, even though it was rather dark by then. We ordered some Slovenian beer and Slovenian sausages. We loved stuffing big fat sausages in our mouths.

After we were finished with the food, which was mediocre, and the beer, which wasn't cold enough—even though on the menu it had said that it was supposed to be as cold as my ex's heart, which is pretty fucking cold—we went inside to pay. There, much to my surprise, on one of the walls hung a large poster of Bukowski with the quote, "Find what you love and let it kill you," which happened to be my favorite quote at the time. (It was only later that I learned that Bukowski hadn't actually said that. It had actually been some fucking country singer instead. And yet somehow it had gotten misattributed as one of Bukowski's most famous quotes . . . May the world fall down on its lies!)

As it was soon too late to take a bus back to the hotel and I sure as shit didn't want to walk back there, we began searching for a bus station. After we finally found the correct one, having first sat down in the wrong one before realizing our mistake by overhearing the loud blather of some nearby British tourists, Morrigan and I had a bit of an argument since I'd been complaining so much during the trip already and it was only day one.

It was indeed true that I had been complaining a lot, but from my point of view, what the hell could I do about it if I simply couldn't stand most of the things that most people were constantly doing in this stupid life of ours, such as flying or walking or waiting in lines?

During the peak of the argument, Morrigan had even suggested buying me a ticket for the next flight back home, which I refused, opting to apologize to her instead.

Eventually the bus arrived, and we drove to the bus station near our hotel. As we walked towards the hotel, we saw that the sky was clear and that there was an immense number of stars visible, perhaps more than I had ever seen. It was so clear due to the alpine region and the lack of light pollution.

We admired the stars for a while and then retired for the evening.

Find what you love and let it kill you.

Charles Bukowski

DAY TWO
TUESDAY

THE NEXT DAY, after having a meagre breakfast that consisted mostly of fried eggs, we went by bus to Vintgar Gorge, where there was a 1.6-kilometer-long walkway next to a river, which ran through a small canyon.

One of the first things I saw in the gorge was a wooden statue of Jesus Christ nailed to a cross. I was beginning to think that Slovenians were very religious people indeed. But then so was most of the world. Regrettably.

As we walked through the gorge, which was packed full of people, there was a family walking in front of us with a bunch of children, some of them being carried in backpacks. Oh yeah, I thought, what a great place to bring a child—on a narrow boardwalk next to a river.

In fact, I couldn't think of a single place it was a good idea to bring a child, including existence, mind you, which was clearly not as good as most people had been led to believe, with its surfeit of disease and suffering and hunger and pain and crime and torture and British tourists.

The reason I despised families with many children in particular was because each child they forced into the world tended to force even more, as did each subsequent generation, which resulted in an exponential growth of new human beings, none of whom asked to be born.

As the philosopher David Benatar has pointed out, assuming each couple has three children, their total descendants over ten generations amount to 88,572 new people. Now that's *a lot* of unnecessary human beings! *A lot* of unnecessary pain and suffering! *A lot* of unnecessary British tourists!

Anyway, one of the children in front of us had clearly shat their pants and it smelled like diarrhea. And of course, the smell wafted over the people walking behind them . . . which was us.

Eventually, when we found a larger section of the boardwalk, we quickly passed by them, only to then see an old lady fall down in front of us, holding up the line. We waited until another old lady that was with her helped her up in slow-motion. Why didn't I help her, you ask? Because why should I? It's not my responsibility. Moreover, if you can't even fucking walk properly, then maybe you shouldn't go to a gorge?

As we walked onwards, admiring the view, there

were also some things that wounded the eye, such as a five-year-old kid with a T-shirt that said, "This is what an influencer looks like," which might as well have said, "This is what someone who should have been aborted looks like."

What wounded Morrigan's eye, however, was a guy with a very visible skin disease. "I'd kill myself if I had that," she told me.

"How shallow," I said. "Besides, there are much better reasons over which to kill yourself. For instance, accidentally dropping your apartment keys whilst trying to unlock the door."

At the end of the gorge there was a waterfall and a bridge that went over it. The bridge was packed full of kids, admiring the rainbow that appeared in the spray of the waterfall. Oh, how I would have loved to have given the kids a little science lesson right then and there!

Hi kids, I would say. Did you know that a rainbow is an optical illusion that is formed when raindrops act like prisms, splitting sunlight into its constituent colors? And did you know that a rainbow is only visible when you are a certain distance away from it since raindrops reflect sunlight only under a certain angle? This means that when you move towards the rainbow, it will actually be new raindrops reflecting a new rainbow, which will always be the same distance from you, meaning you can never actually reach it.

And did you know, kids, that the same principle also applies to happiness? Because happiness, you see, is also an illusion, which will always appear to be the same distance away from you, no matter how much you try to reach it.

After we crossed the bridge, which, unlike for the little kids, was a little scary for me because of my fear of heights, we realized that there was nothing else of interest there. We thus started walking all the way back to the bus stop near the beginning of the gorge.

SINCE THERE WAS some time before the bus arrived, we bought some beers from a nearby cafe and waited.

While we were sipping on the beers, some guys from New Zealand came over and asked me if they could take a photo with me because I happened to be wearing a Duckman T-shirt at the time. Duckman is an animated sitcom that ran in the nineties, which I happened to love, having seen all of its episodes at least five or six times. But when I told the guy this, he told me he wanted the photo merely because his *nickname* was Duckman. He hadn't actually seen the show. And so, my endless wait for meeting another person that cherishes Duckman as much as I do, continues . . . Also, what the fuck kind of nickname is Duckman?

After they left, Morrigan and I, intellectuals that we were and known for our love of children, thought up a new way on how to teach children the alphabet. It went like this: A is for asshole, B is for bitch, C is for cunt, D is for dick, E is for enema, F is for fuck, G is for god, H is for horseshit, I is for imbecile, J is for jerkoff, K is for ketamine, L is for loser, M is for motherfucker, N is for Niger (the country), O is for oral, P is for piss, Q is for queef, R is for ratfucking, S is for shit, T is for tits, U is for uterus, V is for vagina, W is for wanker, X is for xenophobia, Y is for Yankee, and Z is for zoophilia.

Then the bus came. And by that I don't meant that it had an orgasm, I mean that it arrived. Next stop, the oldest castle in Slovenia.

HOLY FUCKIN' SHITBALLS, I thought, as we stepped off the bus. Bled Castle was built right on the edge of a cliff, which offered a mesmerizing view of the town of Bled and the lake below, as well as the numerous mountains in the distance. It was one of the most impressive views I had ever seen—and I'd been to the fucking Himalayas.

We quickly walked through the museum part of the castle, which was as boring as history museums tended to be, and I bought a small bottle of honey liqueur from the gift shop for some inexplicable reason, even though I didn't like honey or liqueur.

Then we went to the cafe and bought some Laško beers. The cafe was right next to the cliff edge, and we found a pretty good spot in the shade from which to admire the view.

There were surprisingly few people around, though I did notice that on one of the tables there were about ten empty beer bottles. Well, with a view like that and a hot day, sitting there and drinking cold beer for hours on end made perfect sense to me. It also made sense in case you wanted to commit suicide since the castle was perched atop a cliff a hundred and thirty meters high.

Whilst I was sipping on my beer, I saw a lizard crawling near our table. It seemed strange to me that it had gotten up so high. I theorized with Morrigan that due to their short lifespans, they must lay their eggs consecutively closer to a higher place in order to finally live there. And so life spreads. Like a virus.

I then noticed that a woman was sitting straight on the edge of the ledge, her feet tangling off. Jesus Christ, I thought. What's wrong with her? Observing such things had always disturbed me on account of my fear of heights. *Especially* when Morrigan did it. Goddamn mirror neurons.

AFTER WE'D HAD enough of the view—although that's like saying "had enough of the heroin"—we walked down the path on the side of the cliff to get down to ground level. We then continued walking alongside the lake until we reached another mountain. This one had something called "summer tobogganing", which were essentially these small vehicles on a rail that went down the side of the mountain. It seemed like fun, so we bought tickets and went up the mountain in a ski lift.

Going up the mountain in the jittery ski lift was scary as fuck for me on account of my fear of heights—or rather, *falling* from heights—since it was about twenty meters from the ground at some points and the ski lift looked old and flimsy as shit.

When we reached the top, we stopped for a moment to take in the view before going on the toboggans, the maximum speed of which was about forty kilometers per hour. I went first. It was a little terrifying initially as it went down the mountain, but I soon grew used to it. The view was great all the way down; I could even see the castle where we came from.

After we had both gotten down, a display showed our speed through the last part of the course, which went through a steep tunnel. Morrigan's was almost twice as high as mine. Goddamn maniac.

It was still real hot outside, so after that we went and had some cold ones in a nearby cafe. And by cold ones, I don't mean corpses, even though I don't necessarily find anything wrong with necrophilia. I mean, they're dead, aren't they? Do you think they give a fuck?

Aside from cold beer, the cafe had a big rotating fan outside that blew cold mist instead of just air. I had never seen such a fan before. It was genius.

ONCE WE WERE done with the beers, we walked back to the lake and bought tickets for a boat ride to the small island on the far side of the lake.

The vessel used for this was a traditional Slovenian boat called a pletna, the design of which dates back to 1590. It was similar in principle to a gondola and used a human motor to row the boat. Our human motor had strong muscular hands, the kind that could easily strangle you to death, as well as a strong resemblance to Rupert Everett. I bet the ladies loved him. Particularly the ones that liked being choked.

The journey across Lake Bled was peaceful and the view was mesmerizing, what with the sunlight glinting off the water like quicksilver, as mountains and Bled Castle loomed large in the distance.

It took us around twenty minutes to arrive at Bled Island, which, like everything else in Bled, had a very imaginative name. Also, it was the only island in Slovenia and of course it *had* to have a fucking church on it.

As I was walking up the steps to the church, I saw a sign which said that you shouldn't walk around the church grounds in a bikini. "Damn," I told Morrigan. "I left my bikini at home. Of course . . . it says nothing about being naked, which after all is the Garden of Eden way."

"Don't forget that little boys don't wear bikinis," said Morrigan.

There wasn't much to do on the island, aside from walking around and making fun of religion. But it was still rather nice and tranquil being there, despite the obvious lack of busty babes in bikinis. I did, however, see a nun at one point. Or perhaps it was a penguin.

Once the boat had taken us back from the island, we felt like wild beasts, ravenous for some food. After a little walking, we found a pizza place where we ordered some beer and two pizzas called "Devil", which, it turned out, was a very popular name in Slovenia for some reason. As I was eating, I accidentally dropped a piece of meat on the ground and watched as some sparrows came and tore it to pieces. The sparrows of Bled were ferocious.

Just as we were finished eating, it suddenly started raining heavily. Since we had no umbrella, we scoured the nearby gift shops until we found one that sold umbrellas. The umbrella we bought was a cheap Chinese piece of shit, like most things in this world. "Goddamn," I said, looking at the shoddy thing as we opened it. "Why's everything so low quality these days? Especially the people."

We were about ready to retire for the day, so we walked to the bus stop. Since there was some time before the bus came, I decided to go and buy a beer from the nearby supermarket. I'd had five so far that day.

Just as I was about to enter the supermarket, a guy in front of it stopped me and said, "Can I ask you something?"

"Sure," I said, thinking, I know where *this* is going.

"Do you like rock music?"

"Yeah. Some."

He told me he was from an Estonian rock band called Illumenium.

Well what are the odds, I thought. Even though I had never heard of them. But then again, I didn't do Estonian culture, baby. At all. Hell, I didn't do culture. Period. I was uncultured. And I aimed to keep it that way.

The guy told me that they were currently collecting money for a tour, whilst he flipped out some CDs for me to browse.

"Interesting artwork," I said, examining the hodgepodge photo collage of an ankh, the Egyptian god Anubis, pyramids, the all-seeing eye, tigers, polar bears, wolves, forests, the tree of life, and a destroyed city. *Extremely* subtle, I thought. These guys must be *deep*.

"Our singer does them himself."

"Yeah, I can see that."

"If you want to buy one, you can pay whatever you want for it."

Damn it, where's a dog turd when you need one? However, since I was in a generous mood, I bought the CD with the least terrible cover art for ten euros. I guess I kind of felt sorry for the guy that he had to lower himself to peddling CDs near a supermarket in fucking Slovenia to make ends meet.

It reminded me of how I had also once wanted to be a rock star. And perhaps subconsciously still did, even though I had replaced that wish with wanting to be a writer instead. So far, I'd had even less success than he did. And yet, had that made me bitter in any way? Why no . . . not at all.

Anyway, after buying the fucking CD, I bought my fucking beer, drank the fucking thing, then the fucking bus came, we went to the fucking hotel, and retired for the fucking day.

DAY THREE
WEDNESDAY

THE NEXT MORNING, after we were finished with breakfast—fucking eggs again—we walked to the bus stop to get into town. However, it turned out that Morrigan had misremembered the bus times, despite me having asked her about five times during breakfast whether she remembered them or not.

As the next bus didn't go for at least an hour, this meant that we had to walk two kilometers into town in the sweltering twenty-eight-degree heat, the sun bombarding us along the way with its disgusting photons. Once again, I hated traveling.

When we finally got to town, I was drenched in sweat. I needed a beer. A *cold* one. Preferably as cold as Vladimir Putin's heart. Or my mother's love.

Fortunately, we quickly found a decent place that was empty. Sitting there, drinking a cold one in the shade whilst cooling down, a little birdy flew on a nearby chair, looking for the meaning of life. It found none. As it scampered off towards the road, I noticed a guy riding a motorcycle and texting on his phone at the same time. Goddamn maniac.

Observing the bar's menu, I saw that it had shots called "Squashed Frog" and "Brain Tumor". I didn't like shots much since they tended to taste terrible and had been the catalysts for some of the worst nights I had ever had, but I always appreciated it when they were named interestingly since it showed a modicum of artistry in an unexpected place.

Once the beer had reinvigorated me enough, we got up to continue on to our first destination for the day, which was to climb a mountain. Before we left, I bought a bottle of water from the bar to go. As the refrigerator outside with the water bottles was locked, we had to wait until the Korean lady behind the counter got the keys. When she finally did, it turned out to be the wrong set of keys. So we had to wait some more until she finally got the correct set of keys. After about fifteen minutes of waiting, I finally got the water.

The trek up the forest-covered mountain was arduous due to the scorching heat and deep incline which occasionally gave me vertigo. The mountain on top of which I had climbed with Morrigan in Tibet was nothing compared to this. And yet, for Morrigan their difficulties were reversed, so perhaps it was largely psychological.

Nevertheless, we eventually managed to make it to

the top, which was 685 meters above sea level. It'd be hard to describe the view without falling into hyperbole but, as an antinatalist might put it, it was as beautiful as an aborted fetus. This, I thought whilst taking in the view, is what Nietzsche must have felt like when he was climbing in the Alps during the 19th century.

After having had enough of the view—although that's like saying "had enough of the crack cocaine"— we continued walking on the forest-covered mountaintop towards another peak. Although some of the road we walked on was extremely unsteady, covered in various sizes of rock, it at least didn't give me any vertigo unlike the rather steep climb to the top. The only thing of interest in the forest that I can recall of was a hut that someone had built out of twigs.

We kept on walking for quite a while, but we must have taken a wrong turn somewhere, because instead of reaching another peak, we ended up just walking down the side of the mountain. Which was fine by me since my legs were like wet noodles at that point and I was beat. I needed another beer.

WE SAT DOWN at the next cafe we found. As we were sipping on our beers, I was suddenly hit with a strong stomachache. I had no idea what caused it, but my mind began racing. Too much beer? Excessive gas? Food poisoning? An ulcer? A tapeworm? Stomach cancer? I was terribly afraid of stomachaches, for I'd already had plenty of them in my life due to my delicate digestion, and I'd once even had one that had been so painful that I literally felt like I was dying. Not that I was afraid of death, mind you; merely the pain that precedes it.

The pain eventually subsided and after we were finished with our beers, we moved on. We bought some beers to go from a nearby store, and walked by the side of the lake towards a swimming area whilst discussing various topics, including how incorrectly the cyberpunk genre has predicted the future, the genius of Bukowski, and—after I saw a guy with Edgar Allan Poe's face tattooed on him walk by—the miserable life of Edgar Allan Poe . . . as well as the stupidity of tattooing someone's face on you.

When we arrived at the swimming area and went to buy a ticket to get in—yeah, you needed a ticket for that—the guy at the counter told us that all the lockers were in use, so we had to risk leaving our stuff outside, which we did.

After we had changed our clothes, we first went down a water slide, which, it turned out, was meant for children. We then went into the water, swam around a bit, and then just floated for a while, holding on to the safety buoys. We also played with each other's genitals a bit underwater.

Although the water was warm and the view was

great, with Bled Castle on a precipice right above the swimming area, we soon decided to leave as I wasn't a big fan of just laying around in water all day. After all, I wasn't a goddamn fish. Hadn't been one for hundreds of millions of years. Unfortunately.

WHILST WALKING AWAY from the beach, we noticed a small abandoned red brick building nearby. The fence was broken so we stepped inside. It must have been a lovely building once, I thought, as I stood in its dilapidated guts. Yet now it lay in ruins, just like everything would in time.

I later learned that the building, which had once been a villa, had belonged to a Swiss naturopath from the 19th century who had moved to Bled because he'd had diarrhea—I shit you not—and thought that the way to cure all diseases, including diarrhea, was to stand naked in the sun for long periods of time, which he often did. In fact, it was thanks to him that Bled became a popular health tourism destination in the 19th century among other standing-naked-in-the-sun enthusiasts—which, by the way, the locals were not exactly thrilled with. While pseudoscience may not be true, it is at least often entertaining.

After moving away from the abandoned villa, we started getting hungry, so we began searching for a restaurant, preferably one which served authentic Slovenian food, whatever that was. We soon found one on the map that wasn't far off. On the road there, we were surprised to see sheep fenced off near the street, and Morrigan stopped for a moment to pet a stray cat.

AFTER WE SAT down on the restaurant terrace, my stomachache suddenly came back with a vengeance. Nevertheless, I decided to eat. Perhaps the food would help, I irrationally thought.

The food in the restaurant was bland and boring. Gordon Ramsay wouldn't have liked it. Also, neither my salmon nor Morrigan's veal seemed like "authentic Slovenian food" in any way, whatever that was (probably something disgusting).

But at least there was some entertainment. When a person next to us had temporarily left her seat, a sparrow had swiftly flown onto her table and started eating her food. Everybody in the restaurant was observing it as it was struggling with a noodle, nobody daring to chase it off. It got a few good pieces before scampering off as the person came back to the table.

My stomachache got even worse after I finished eating, so I went to the bathroom, hoping to take a shit in order to alleviate the pain, but all I managed was a fart . . . which didn't help much.

When I got back, Morrigan told me that she had seen a black cat catch a small mouse or a bird near the restaurant. I told her I wanted to leave and she left to pay. I then went looking for the cat, ultimately finding two black cats in a nearby alleyway who were indeed playing with some kind of small dead animal.

My stomachache got worse and worse, so I had to start walking more slowly. Soon, I also needed to pee, as did Morrigan, so we began searching for a bathroom.

At first, we went to a gas station, but the bathroom there was locked. We then walked to a nearby supermarket, which had a bathroom with two stalls. The first stall I entered had feces smeared all over the walls, ground, and toilet bowl—god only knows what went down there—so I took the other one.

After that we sat down on a bench in the supermarket, waiting for the bus back to the hotel. I also went and bought some yogurt drinks, which I gulped down in a feeble attempt at alleviating my stomachache. It seemed I was becoming as irrational as the guy who had stood in the sun too long.

By the time the bus came, my stomachache had largely subsided—though I doubt it was because of the yogurt—so instead of going directly to the hotel, we decided to first visit a large river which ran near the foot of the mountain visible from our hotel room.

We got off the bus and walked through the small village towards the river. On the way there we noticed that the village was infested everywhere with Spanish slugs as big as penises.

The river was calm, reflecting the clouds in the sky, and the nearby mountain had mist creeping down its side. It was picturesque. Although we didn't have it in us anymore for another hike, we decided to take a quick look.

The mountain passage, which was surrounded by trees, was covered in darkness; it looked ominous. We walked through it until we came to a small field where a young deer was standing. It raised its head and looked at us for a while before walking away. It was a strange omen, I'd have thought, had I believed in such things.

On the way back, I noticed a church and a large cross on top of a mountain in the distance. "God is dead," Nietzsche had once said. "But given the way of men, there may still be caves for thousands of years in which his shadow will be shown." Or, as is the case, mountains.

Back at the hotel, I took a shower and listened to a few Illumenium songs. Not from their CD, mind you, but from their Spotify. Because who the hell uses CDs these days? The songs were okay—definitely better than the artwork on their albums—but nothing to write home about. Nothing special.

We then watched some episodes of *It's Always Sunny in Philadelphia* on my laptop and drank beer. One of the episodes had Mac and Charlie wanting to

make a movie and then Dennis came on as a pro-
ducer, suggesting that it should feature Dolph
Lundgren as a scientist and include full penetration
sex scenes. I liked Dolph Lundgren, science, and full
penetration, so it seemed like a pretty good idea to
me.

However, if given the chance, I would have per-
sonally made something a little bit darker and more
controversial. Perhaps, for instance, a realistic serial
killer movie where the camera follows a serial killer
as he explicitly rapes young women and then gouges
out their eyes and rapes their eyeholes with his erect
cock?

DAY FOUR
THURSDAY

IN THE MORNING, or *asubuhi* as they say in Swahili, we ate breakfast—goddamn eggs again—and then got ready to leave for another hotel in the capital city of Slovenia.

I was already annoyed at the prospect of having to first go by bus to Bled, then take another bus to Ljubljana, and then finally a taxi to our hotel, which was about five kilometers from the city center.

To make matters worse, it turned out that Morrigan had not checked on how to get around Ljubljana, which I assumed she had done. I had left this up to her because my sense of direction was shit and I hated planning such things. Indeed, what I hated most about traveling was perhaps the getting from one place to another, which tended to be a confusing and annoying waste of time.

After we had checked out of the hotel, we walked to the bus station. The bus was late. I scratched off a small growth on my neck, while waiting, which began bleeding. I had forgotten to bring any bandages, so I held a tissue paper over it.

It still bled when we arrived in Bled, so I went to the store to buy some bandages. I applied the bandage in the same shit-covered bathroom that I had visited the day before. As we were walking away from the store, I suddenly remembered that we also didn't have any water, so I went back and bought some.

We walked to the Bled bus station and started waiting for the bus to Ljubljana. I read a couple of short stories from Bukowski whilst waiting. One was about Bukowski's alter ego Henry Chinaski having a boxing match with Hemingway, and another was a western titled "Stop Looking at my Tits, Mister" which, I guess, was about rape. Anyway, they were both pretty good. But then again, Bukowski could write about taking a shit and make it sound interesting. Which is what great writing is all about. Not plot since real life doesn't have any plot; only meaningless escapism does.

The bus was fifteen minutes late. It seemed that everything was in Bled. Moreover, when it arrived, we still had to wait fifteen minutes more, on top of the half an hour we had already waited, before the bus finally began moving. It often felt as though life consisted mostly of waiting for the interesting things to happen, which rarely did.

The bus ride was boring, as bus rides tended to be.

Unless you had alcohol and the bus had a working toilet, neither of which was the case here. I passed the time by reading Bukowski and occasionally looking out the window, not that there was much to look at, aside from some distant mountains here and there.

Goddamn I hated waiting. Waiting for a bus. Waiting for a train. Waiting for a taxi. Waiting for a plane. Waiting to get to a destination. Waiting for something interesting to happen. Some people tolerated the waiting; I didn't.

And when something *finally* happened, it was rarely as good as you expected it to be because you had made it seem much better in your head while you were waiting. Moreover, since we tended to borrow joy from the future in order to make the present more palatable, this made the already unlikely future even less enjoyable when it arrived. If it ever did.

WHEN WE ARRIVED in Ljubljana, we took the first taxi we found to our hotel, which turned out to be much closer than what it had seemed like on the map.

We learned from the hotel clerk, who was a very helpful and nice guy, that it took only fifteen minutes to get to the city center by bus and that the bus stop was right around the corner. He also gave us detailed instructions on how to get around Ljubljana, along with a preloaded bus card that we had to refill with money and return to him before checking out, as well as a map where he scribbled some helpful details.

It probably seems as though I'm an unpleasant person—which may be true to an extent—but I'm also very kind to those who are kind to me, which in my experience is extremely rare, and I truly appreciated the hotel clerk's helpfulness.

The hotel room itself was also rather nice, much better than I had expected it to be. It even had proper air-conditioning, unlike the previous one. My fear of having to stay at another shitty hotel ran by Chinese immigrants in the middle of nowhere was put to rest.

After we were settled in, Morrigan and I decided to book a tour for the next day in an underground cave system, which was some ways out of the city. Planning it was a nightmare though, as we had to check what time the tour began, what time the bus went from the hotel, what time the bus went from the city center, what time the bus went from the caves to a nearby castle which was included in the ticket price, what time it went back to the caves, and finally what time it went back to the city center, from which we *still* had to take yet another bus back to the hotel. Goddamn shit that's a lot of driving and waiting!

ONCE WE WERE done with booking the tour, we went to the store to buy some beer. *A lot* of beer. It was quite a long way to the nearest store and Morrigan nearly got a heat stroke whilst walking there since it was so goddamn hot outside.

Whilst walking, we also noticed how Ljubljana didn't look *nearly* as good as Bled did. In fact, it looked just like any other semi-large and faceless city, full of trash and graffiti. But then again, all cities *were* basically the same. Ugly concrete jungles where a bunch of self-obsessed semi-advanced apes were frolicking around, hallucinating something they call society. Why anyone would want to travel between these nearly identical and overpopulated concrete jungles was a mystery to me.

After we got back to the hotel and put the beer in the fridge, we started walking towards a nearby restaurant since—surprise, surprise—we were hungry again. Hell, I guess life *was* mostly about eating. And, of course, waiting.

Unfortunately, the restaurant was closed, so we had to walk all the way back to where we came from. And then we walked some more to another restaurant, which, it turned out, was also closed. And when we walked to yet another restaurant, believe it or not, it was also closed. I was beginning to think that there was some kind of cosmic conspiracy at work against me.

Having walked for hours by that point, we settled on some burgers from a shitty-looking fast-food joint that we had passed before—the only place we could find that was open—and went back to the hotel.

The burger was soggy and disgusting, one of the worst things I had eaten in a while. We chased them down with some beers and watched a few episodes of *Sunny in Philadelphia* on the hotel TV, which I had hooked my laptop to, before retiring for the day.

When I got up during the night to pee, my stomach hurt quite badly again, no doubt on account of the abomination I had eaten a short while ago. One who eats well, also shits well, as Marian Dora said. And I did not shit well that night. Not at all.

To make matters worse, once I had emptied my rectum of liquid shit, I couldn't fall asleep afterwards. Instead I lay awake in bed for at least three more hours, contemplating upon the many missed opportunities of my life—that I didn't fuck that Swedish chick for instance—or the ugliness of existence or the poetry of pornography or the necessity of alcohol or some such shit like that before finally dozing off.

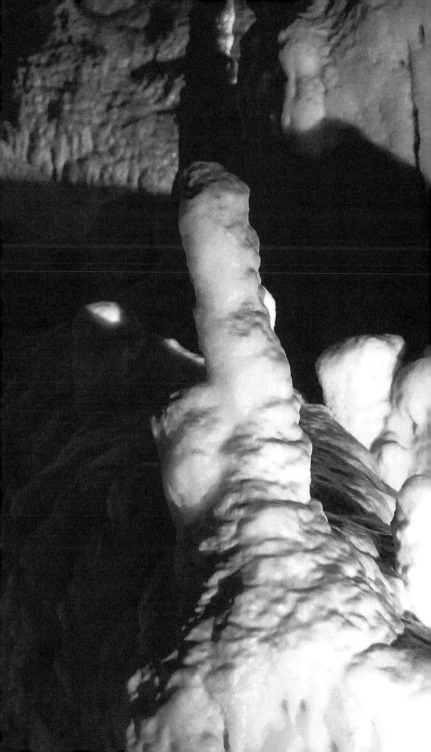

DAY FIVE
FRIDAY

WHEN WE GOT to the breakfast area in the morning, it seemed that all the good stuff was already gone. Not that there had been much of it to begin with by the looks of it.

Once we had both had a shower, we went by bus to the city center. Once there, we located the central bus station, initially going the wrong way for a while before eventually realizing our mistake.

The bus station was small and cramped and had long fucking lines. After we had waited in the line for a while, it was clear that it wasn't moving, so we decided to see if we could buy the tickets from the bus instead. We located the bus, and although it was almost full, we were lucky enough to get two tickets. And then off we were towards the city of Postojna and its underground cave complex.

There was a heavy downpour of rain for a while as the bus drove on the highway, which soon subsided. To make time pass, Morrigan and I started reading entries from James Randy's *An Encyclopedia of Claims, Frauds, and Hoaxes of the Occult and Supernatural*, which I happened to have on my smartphone. Here's a few of the entries that I found amusing:

ADAM—In the *Bible*, the First Man. He was mated to Eve, the First Woman. Their sons were Cain and Abel. In a Talmudic legend, however, Adam's first wife was Lilith and she bore him demons. Parenthood, it seems, is an uncertain art fraught with various problems.

ADONI—A title substituted by the Hebrews for "Jehovah" to avoid pronouncing or even writing the latter word, which is supposed to be so holy and powerful that it brings punishment upon the one who utters it. No evidence exists that any such calamity visits a transgressor, and in fact the reader may repeat the word endlessly out loud without fear of penalty. However, people may think you strange, and no guarantees are given.

ANCIENT ASTRONAUTS—There is a theory that thousands of years ago, civilizations from other star systems visited Earth and gave early Man information to assist in his development. The idea seems to be that folks used to be pretty slow-witted and had to have help to develop such clever stuff as the wheel, bricks, and cudgels.

Evidence has been offered by many writers, particularly by best-seller Von Däniken and none of it is convincing when the actual facts are determined and examined even casually. The theory is presently promoted by tabloid newspapers, sensationalist journals, UFO periodicals, and other fringe-science entities, but holds little interest for serious researchers.

WHEN WE GOT to the caves, as was to be expected, there were lots of tourists everywhere. But this didn't bother me as much as it usually would have since I had already anticipated it due to the popularity of the place.

Besides, the caves themselves were quite amazing, taking us first by a small train and then on foot a hundred meters underground. I was mesmerized by the beautiful cave formations all along the way.

Nearly everything in the caves was covered in stalactites and stalagmites, many of them several meters long. It took about a hundred years for one centimeter of stalactite to form, which meant that the caves were the product of hundreds of thousands or even millions of years. There was even a stalagmite that was shaped like a cock—a hundred-thousand-year-old cock!

Also, what I found fascinating was that the caves did not experience any seasons, which meant that it was ten degrees inside all year round. The contrast between the sweltering heat outside was staggering indeed and made many a tourist nipple erect.

As I explored the cave system, I began wondering about the black coating covering large parts of it. I later read that the black coating in some parts consisted of microorganisms. In other parts from soot deposited by old petrol locomotives. And yet in other parts from a huge inferno that blazed in the caves for seven days during World War II after the Slovenian anti-Nazi resistance movement destroyed the aircraft fuel that the Nazis had been storing in there.

AFTER WE HAD exited the caves, we went to a nearby vivarium, which was built inside another, smaller cave, and hosted some of the exotic species that lived in the larger cave complex.

The star animal there was the olm, which was a blind cave-dwelling aquatic salamander that could survive without food for up to ten years and had a lifespan of up to one hundred years. And, as with many other interesting species, humans had driven them to the brink of extinction.

We then grabbed a bite to eat and had a beer at some shitty fast-food joint. For me, there were few things more magical than a cold beer on a hot day.

Afterwards, we took a bus to the nearby Predjama Castle, which is built partly inside a cave. The castle had apparently been the home of a robber baron during the 15ᵗʰ century before it was destroyed during a siege and later rebuilt. The castle was small, though somewhat impressive. Unfortunately, it was packed to the brim with tourists, which made the tiny castle hallways frustrating to navigate. The more people there were at any given place, the more disgusting that place became for me, regardless of how beautiful it might have otherwise been. And yes, that includes planet Earth.

After the castle, we took a bus back to Postojna and then waited for a bus back to Ljubljana. When the bus arrived, everyone rushed towards it like animals.

ON THE BUS, Morrigan and I got to talking about the pros and cons of traveling. As far as I was concerned, since eating, drinking, and talking to stupid people tended to be the same all over the world, the only *good* reason to travel were the unique sights one saw along the way.

Although I hadn't traveled extensively, I had been to a few unique places over time thanks to Morrigan, such as the Himalayan mountains, the Potala Palace, and the non-tourist part of the Great Wall of China. I had been inside an underground nuclear missile silo in Ukraine, and I had stayed eight days in Chernobyl, which both Morrigan and I loved, largely due to its lack of tourists and commercialized bullshit.

But truly memorable places were few and far in between and often difficult or costly to go to. Unless you were rich that is, which neither of us were by any stretch of the imagination. And of course there were many places which only seemed good on pictures.

When I visited the famous Neuschwanstein Castle in Germany, for instance, it didn't seem so much a fairy tale as more of a nightmare. Souvenir shops and fast-food stands littered the sides of the road that took you up the mountain, on which hundreds of semi-conscious tourists were shuffling along, stuffing their faces with food, whilst taking hundreds of pointless photos that they would never look at, while their annoying little kids, who couldn't tell a castle from a fucking crack house, were zigzagging behind them, getting in everyone's way.

And once you arrived in the castle courtyard, you saw endless lines of people waiting like cattle in front of electronic gates which only let a certain amount of people through at certain intervals. And when you finally got inside the castle you were only allowed to stay five minutes in each room before being pushed through to the next one like on a factory line, the whole visit lasting only thirty minutes. How magical indeed!

Whether it was all worth it in the end was open to question. To most people it clearly was. But I didn't really care what most people thought considering the human being's capacity for self-delusion. And yet, I also *wanted* to have traveled since I didn't want to be boring. Even though traveling itself was often boring.

ONCE THE BUS arrived back in the city, we started walking towards a museum of illusions. To get to it, we crossed several bridges over a river which ran through the city. The river was brown and looked like an open sewer.

The museum itself wasn't too bad I suppose, even though the ticket was too expensive and everything in it had a sort of worn-out look. And of course, as was to be expected, it didn't have the biggest illusion of them all—*that life was worth living*.

We then began searching for a restaurant. The first place we went into, which was called Sarajevo 86, was packed. In fact, people were *actually* waiting in line for other people to finish eating so they could sit down in the restaurant. My God, I thought, looking at these fools. What is wrong with people? How the fuck can they stand standing in fucking lines so much?

Luckily, we soon found a Mexican restaurant

nearby which had a couple of vacant tables outside. Shortly thereafter, it started pouring rain so hard that it seemed as though God himself was taking a piss. The restaurant umbrella kept us dry. Mostly. Then came the thunder and lightning, which I had always enjoyed. I once had an ex who was scared of thunder. But then again, she was only ten years old. At least mentally.

The food that we were served was extremely good for a change. The best I'd had in a long time. After we were finished with the food and beer, we also downed two shots of tequila at the bar counter. Because you can't go into a Mexican restaurant without drinking tequila—it's against the law. I don't know what brand it was as I told the waiter to give us the most popular one, but its taste, oddly, was sweet and good, unlike the usual tequila which tastes like rancid shit.

While waiting to pay, I noticed how a wine glass was rolling around on its side on a waiter's platter before finally shattering onto the ground. Ah, entropy, my old friend.

After paying, we went to the bus station, which fortunately was close by. It was still raining ducks and frogs and the streets had turned into rivers. When we got to the hotel, we took off our wet shoes, had a few beers and then went to sleep.

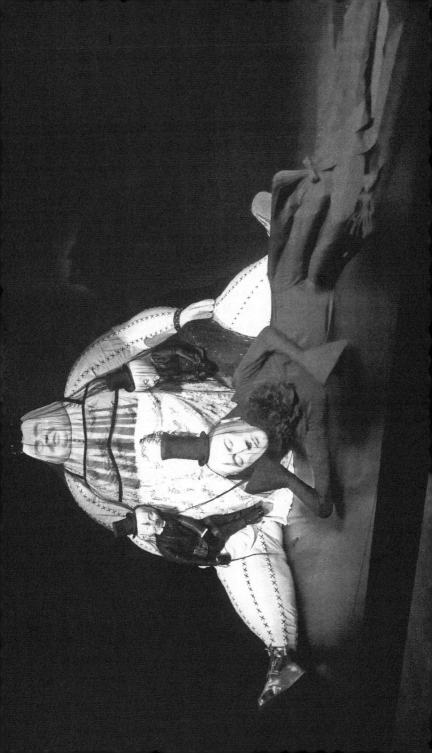

...OSVINSKI ...SOLSKI
...ENTER LJUBLJANA
SOLSKA DELAVNICA HOTEL
BE... PREUREJENA V
CASU 40 ... NICE KPJ
SEPTEMBRA 19...9

DAY SIX
SATURDAY

WE WOKE UP a bit earlier the next morning in order to make sure that there was more food left in the breakfast area. But the extra food there looked disgusting, so I didn't even touch it. Besides, the room was full of people and their stupid and annoying little children who kept running around and screaming. There was not a more revolting sound in the entire universe for me than the sound of a child screaming. I couldn't wait to get out of there.

We were thinking of where to go on our last few days in Ljubljana, but it seemed that there wasn't much to see in the city. All the interesting things had been in Bled and we had already visited most of them. We finally decided to go see the castle in the center of the city, which was on most pictures of Ljubljana.

When we went to the bus stop, it turned out that Morrigan had looked at the wrong bus timetable. Nevertheless, a buss soon came. When we stepped on the bus, however, the driver chased us away, as though we were children. It seemed it wasn't the "proper" time to enter yet. The proper time to enter, in fact, was five minutes later. Goddamn bastard.

When we got near the castle, we wanted to go up the mountain in a funicular, which was essentially a glass box that went up the side of the mountain on a rail. I bought tickets for the funicular and the castle. As usual, there was a long line before we got on and then they packed us in like sardines. The ride was over in one minute and was utterly underwhelming.

At the top, I needed to go to the bathroom. There appeared to be only one in the entire castle. Of course, it cost money, despite me already having bought the castle tickets. It seemed you needed to have a ticket for pretty much anything in Slovenia. In the end, however, the ticket machine wasn't even working so I just jumped over the gate.

The castle, as was to be expected, was over-crowded. Lots of stupid fucking people with their stupid fucking children, all of them taking stupid fucking pictures of stupid fucking things, preferring to watch reality through the stupid fucking screens of their stupid fucking phones, instead of experiencing it with their goddamned eyes, the stupid motherfuck-ers!

In one of the first rooms that we entered there was a copper plate where one was free to engrave whatever one wanted, so I engraved a swastika and a dick on it and Morrigan engraved "FUCK YOU".

What? It was *ironic*.

After we went through the history portion of the castle, which was dead boring—oh look, fucking spear tips again—we went up the castle tower. Or to be more precise, Morrigan went up the castle tower. My fear of heights, as usual, only allowed me to go up about halfway before it got too disturbing.

In the exhibition area of the castle there happened to be an exhibition of costumes designed by some guy named Alan Hranitelj. I rarely cared for exhibitions, but the costumes this guy designed were insane, like something out of a nightmare version of Alice in Wonderland. The costumes were extremely detailed and surreal and had weird and extravagant geometric patterns. Some also had giant eyes and ears and lips sewn on. They seemed like the kind of thing Marilyn Manson might wear (perhaps while abusing one of his girlfriends).

There were also some cloth sculptures from the guy. One of them was called "Templar" and it looked like a nightmare version of a centaur, which would have been a fitting guard for the gates of hell. A very elegant hell I might add.

Then there was a giant fat wife on whose thighs two small old people sat as her fed-up husband lay on the ground in front of her. Gee, I wonder what the symbolism there might be.

My favorite, however, was the mantis in a bride's costume that was titled "At Your Own Risk". Indeed, I thought, as I had never understood the point of marriage, which seemed like a bunch of nonsensical and obsolete ancient bullshit to me. Or as my favorite comedian Doug Stanhope put it:

> If marriage didn't exist, would you invent it? Would you go, "Baby, this shit we got together? It's so good we gotta get the government in on this shit. We can't just share this commitment between us. We need judges and lawyers involved in this shit, baby. It's hot!"

AFTER THE CASTLE, we went to see the "Dragon Bridge" of Ljubljana, which was a bridge with some small dragon statues on it. It was utterly fucking pointless.

We then went to the oldest skyscraper in the city, which had been built in the thirties and at the time was the ninth tallest building in Europe. Supposedly, it had an Art Deco architecture, which I was a fan of.

Well, there wasn't much Art Deco left, if there ever had been, but the view from the cafe on top was quite nice so we decided to stay for a while and have some beers. I felt a small sense of vertigo sitting near the edge of the balcony, but it was manageable. Besides, it seemed that the more beer I drank, the less I felt it.

Inspired by the surroundings, I started telling Morrigan how my fear of heights usually manifests.

"Essentially, when I'm high up somewhere and there's a ledge nearby where I could *theoretically* fall from, I begin feeling as though the building is slightly moving or vibrating. I also feel I might accidentally slip and fall off it, or that someone might push me"—which, considering my "charming" personality, was perhaps not entirely unlikely"—and at times I even get the feeling that the building might collapse right under me. Which, of course, is almost impossible. Unless you're in India, that is."

"Interesting . . ." Morrigan said.

"I know it's all very irrational and silly but try telling my stupid fucking brain that."

ONCE WE WERE done with our beers, we left the cafe and went for a walk in the largest park in the city, which had a small mountain in the middle of it.

There was a bronze statue near the entrance of the park of a nude boy playing flute. We rubbed his little dick for good luck before moving on. We then passed by the botanical garden that was in the park territory, which, alas, turned out to be closed.

Whilst walking deeper into the park between the thick forest, at one point I saw a small rodent scurrying by. We soon left the beaten path and, after finding a more secluded spot, I suggested to Morrigan that we should have sex there, to which she agreed. She rarely said no to sex. I pulled her pants down and started fucking her from behind, constantly on the lookout to make sure that nobody saw us. It didn't take long for me to come since fucking in public was a rush, and when I did I came on her ass.

After sex, we continued walking in the park for a while until we came to an abandoned building. It looked intriguing, so we hopped the fence and wandered inside. It looked like the building had been abandoned for a while since it was crumbling all over and plants were growing inside of it.

We explored the second and third floors, as well as the terrace. When we entered the basement, however, it became slightly unnerving for me because of the darkness and because I kept picturing how a homeless person might suddenly jump out of the shadows and stab us, or how a gang of punks might take us hostage and rape Morrigan whilst forcing me to watch. Yeah, I had probably watched too many movies.

Of course, nothing happened. But the place *was* interesting. It was quite large and even had elevator shafts. It reminded me of the abandoned buildings Morrigan and I had visited in Pripyat. There were also some bloody handprints in the bathroom and on the walls, which was *presumably* just red paint from some vandal with a dark sense of humor.

I later read about the hotel on the internet. It was called Hotel Bellevue and was built in 1909. It was sold several times, eventually ending up as a dance club. Then, several fires left the building in disrepair. It had been a very popular place once, yet now it lay abandoned, its onetime beauty having decayed into ruin. As it is with all things in the end.

AFTER WE LEFT the ruins, I felt hungry enough to eat a horse. And as it happens, there was a place nearby that sold horse meat burgers, which both of us were eager to try.

The burgers were tasty, and the beer was cold, as it should be. As we were eating, Morrigan and I got to talking about immigrants and refugees, a topic that was often in the news at the time. Both of us agreed that educated immigrants should be welcome in all countries, whereas criminals and welfare parasites should not, for all countries already had enough of those. And if the latter didn't like their countries, then too bad—it wasn't another country's problem.

Why should a country want some fraudster from Nigeria or some fundamentalist from Syria who wants a better life? Whereas they would have to be insane to turn down a brain surgeon from India, for instance, or an engineer from Pakistan. It wasn't a question of race or religion. It was a question of whether the immigrant was going to be harmful or beneficial for the country in question. Because why on earth would a country want to harm itself? The liberals and conservatives had made it seem as though it was a question of all or nothing, whereas the truth, as always, lay somewhere in between.

A thunderstorm suddenly developed outside and there was heavy rain, thunder, and lightning, just like the day before. As we found storms entertaining, we ordered two more beers and watched the show. When the storm finally subsided, we left.

IN BETWEEN OUR wanderings that day, Morrigan had managed to book a tour to the Julian Alps in the Triglav National Park for the following day. I was thankful for that as otherwise there would have been nothing to do on our last full day in Slovenia.

There were a few things we had to do first though. We had to take out some cash to pay for the tour, recharge our bus card and buy a new one, and finally buy some food for the next morning since we were going to leave too early to have breakfast at the hotel.

Finding an ATM was easy. Finding a machine that sold bus cards and let you recharge them took a while. Finding a place that sold food took even longer since on Saturday everything seemed to be closed in Ljubljana for some stupid reason.

Eventually, we found a gas station where we bought some sandwiches and beer. I noticed that the gas station also sold candy called "Negro" but I didn't buy any; I didn't like licorice.

Then, when we went back to the bus station, we found two shops that were both open, as well as the goddamn ticket machine that we had previously been searching for half an hour. Now that just pissed me the fuck off. Why couldn't there be clear instructions? Why couldn't things make sense? Why were some shops closed while others remained open? Why did some ticket machines do what they were supposed to while others did not? Why was the world so fucking inconsistent?

While waiting for the bus, I went to one of the nearby shops and bought some more beers, opening one right away in order to calm myself down. I downed it just as the bus arrived.

In the hotel we had a few more beers, watched some episodes of *Sunny in Philadelphia*, and soon went to bed since we had to wake up at seven in the morning the next day.

I hated waking up early in the morning, preferring to sleep until noon like Descartes, Bukowski, and all the other geniuses. Still, I thought we were lucky to have gotten the tour as we had booked it only one day in advance.

2,59

Pionir

ODŽAČAR GRLA

NEGRO®

1,58

2,35

And the first team
to complete all three levels
wins the game.

DAY SEVEN
SUNDAY

THE TOUR VAN picked us up shortly after seven in the morning. It was a small vehicle, so thankfully there weren't going to be many people.

First, we drove back to Bled to pick up a few more passengers, about whom I can hardly recall a single detail, and then we started towards the Julian Alps. The mountainous road towards the Alps reminded me of Northern Norway, which I had visited a long time ago.

We stopped at a railroad station where we were going to board a car train—a train that transports cars—that was going to take us through a mountain tunnel.

Since we had to wait a while for the train to arrive, Morrigan and I bought some coffee and energy drinks and explored the station a bit. Inside the station building, we learned that the tunnel was about six kilometers long, more than a hundred years old, and had been built by prisoners of war.

The tour guide also told us that the engineer that had been responsible for measuring the tunnel committed suicide when the holes bored from each side of the mountain met and it turned out that there had been a small mismeasurement.

When we drove onto the car train and it took us inside the tunnel, it was pitch black. As was the humor of our tour guide, who told us, "Well, this is it, my victims." And, as if to add to the effect, he didn't turn on the interior lights throughout the darkness.

After we exited the tunnel, the train drove on for some time through a valley between the mountains, with many small bridges and short tunnels along the way. It was a fascinating and unusual journey, being on the car train.

When we arrived at the train station, the tour van exited the car train and continued on driving until we reached Triglav National Park, which was the only national park in Slovenia. Whilst we drove, the guide pointed out a mountaintop in the shape of a woman, which he said the Slovenians called Sleeping Beauty. He said the reason they knew that it's a woman was because a part of the mountain looked like her boobs.

It did indeed, I thought, observing her sharp peaks. Though not enough to get excited over. Unless the triangular boobs of Lara Croft from the first Tomb Raider game turned you on, that is.

OUR FIRST STOP was near the Tolmin Gorges, where we walked over Devil's Bridge, which was suspended sixty meters in the air. The walkway on the side of the cliff took us to the bottom of the gorge. I felt slight vertigo at times due to the steep edges of the cliff, but I managed.

The gorge was beautiful. It was bigger and there were much fewer people around than in the gorge we had visited on our second day. At the bottom of it was a waterfall that fell between two cliffs and sort of looked like the Batcave. Tadpoles swam in its waters.

Whilst walking back to the tour van, our guide told us that the Austro-Hungarian Empire and the Italians had fought the biggest war ever fought on a mountain in this area. He showed us the cramped caves where the soldiers had lived.

He also told us the following joke: A genie asked a guy what he wants. "To be rich and famous," the guy said. The guy then went to sleep. After he woke up the next day, his friend asked him, "So, Ferdinand, are you ready to go to Sarajevo?"

Good joke, I thought.

We then drove on for a short while before stopping at Soča valley where we went on another hike. Right away, there was a rather long suspension bridge high above the Soča river, which we had to cross. I was a bit hesitant at first, observing as the others walked over it, but I finally managed to cross it.

THE NEXT STOP on our schedule was to go rafting. It was something I had never done before and it seemed a little too extreme for me, but I decided to give it a shot, especially since Morrigan seemed enthusiastic about it.

After the tour van dropped us off near another part of the Soča river, we were given wetsuits and told to change into them either right there or in the van. Morrigan went to change in the van, but I got naked right there in front of everybody. "Hell yeah, this is Europe!" a guy near me commented.

Then a rafting instructor explained us the rules. He also informed us that the river was class three in difficulty and that the maximum was class five. That's quite a bit for a beginner, I thought.

I was a bit nervous at the beginning after the raft got on its way, especially after the instructor ordered us to jump into the freezing river at the start of the journey so that we'd "get used to falling off the raft." But the nervousness soon disappeared, largely, I suppose, due to the adrenaline. From that point on, it was a rush every second of the way, especially when we hit the rapids.

At one point, we stopped on the side of the river and made a slide from the raft by placing it sideways on a boulder. We then jumped from the cliff onto the raft and slid into the river. I did it once, which was quite enough for me, and Morrigan went twice, once headfirst. We also stopped near a larger boulder where people climbed on and then jumped off it into the waters below. The drop was about eight meters, which was a bit too much for me and Morrigan, so we stayed in the raft.

The journey had so far been without incident, until the raft hit the most severe rapids of the river and Morrigan and two others suddenly went flying off the raft into the waters that were rushing downstream. The instructor swiftly caught Morrigan, and one of them managed to climb back on his own, but I had to save this old lady who was quickly going down the river towards a cliff with our raft going in the same direction. I managed to pull her up into the raft just in time before she would have been crushed against the rock. The experience had felt like a scene from some Hollywood movie. My blood was pumping.

After that, the ride was over. We carried the raft, which was damn heavy, to the van and got dressed. We were then driven to a nearby town where we had lunch at an Italian place. I ordered a big pizza with sausages and chili and Morrigan ordered cannelloni. Of course, we also drank a few beers.

AFTER LUNCH WAS over, we went on a hiking trail, the most difficult one thus far. In fact, I had to abandon it before reaching the end as it turned into essentially walking on the side of a cliff whilst holding on to a cable, which was clearly too much for me and my goddamn fear of heights. The old lady who owed me her life was the only other person in our group that turned back. I told Morrigan to be careful as she went on. I then wandered around the area alone, admiring the view of the distant mountains, as well as a nearby waterfall, whilst waiting for the others to get back.

After the hike, the van stopped at Vršič Pass, which was the highest point in our trip, with an elevation of 1600 meters above sea level. We got out of the van and admired the view, which was magnificent indeed. Two dogs were also running around the area, whom Morrigan and I admired almost as much as the view. I loved dogs, you see; I only hated humans—and yes, that includes myself. Observing the dogs, I wondered whether they had any realization of how special the view was. One of them casually taking a piss in a nearby bush answered that question.

We continued driving down the other side of the pass before stopping on the side of the road near a small Russian Orthodox chapel built out of wood. The tour guide told us that it had been built to honor the hundred Russian prisoners of war that died during World War I whilst building the road that took us over the mountain pass. He said that even Vladimir Putin had visited the chapel not long ago and that it was an olive branch for Russian-Slovenian relations.

I didn't see how a small wooden church remedied

forcing a thousand Russian POWs to build a road in the mountains for a year, which ended up killing a hundred of them, but then people did love their symbols, didn't they? I guess they were symbol minded.

We drove on a bit before stopping near Prisojnik Mountain where the tour guide told us a folktale about the mountain: There once was a maiden who could foretell the fates of unborn babies. One day she prophesized about a boy who would grow up to become a hunter and catch the fabled Goldenhorn, a mythical goat whose golden horns were the key to a treasure hidden in the Triglav mountains. Infuriated that she foresaw the death of the Goldenhorn, her siblings placed a curse on her, which transformed her into a part of the mountain.

Like most folktales, it made no sense. However, I could see that there was indeed a "face" of some sort on the mountainside, which of course was merely an example of pareidolia—the human tendency to perceive meaningful images in random patterns.

My own eyes, in fact, saw an additional figure on the mountainside, which looked far more sinister; it resembled a human skull.

OUR LAST STOP was a quick one near a small lake at a ski resort. Whilst the others were talking about the sights they had seen during the day, Morrigan and I observed the ducks swimming in the lake. It was about eight in the evening and slowly getting dark. I was so tired at this point that all I wanted was to sleep.

When we started driving back, we took another route, so that we didn't have to use the car train this time around. Morrigan attempted to do the check-in for our flights during the ride, but it turned out that the plane had been overbooked and online check-in wasn't available, meaning we had to get to the airport early the next day.

The guide dropped the others off in Bled and then the three of us continued driving towards Ljubljana. During the hour-long drive, we talked about crypto-currency, banks, immigration, where each of us worked—it turned out that the guide was actually a computer engineer who did the tours as a hobby—the Slovenian economy—which wasn't doing so great in his opinion—and communism. He told us that many people in Slovenia were better off with communism than they were now. This seemed like a load of shit to me, but since I didn't know anything about Slovenian history, I didn't argue the point.

When we were nearing Ljubljana, the guide asked us whether we were hungry, which we were indeed. So he kindly offered to drive us to a fast-food place which sold some Balkan thing called börek.

Once there, we had to wait in line for a while until we were finally able to buy two to go. The guide then drove us to our hotel, for which we were extremely thankful, for it was almost eleven in the evening.

Before he left, he offered us some advice about mountain climbing. "Take plenty of warm clothes with you," he said. "Because if a storm suddenly develops, which is common here in the summers, that twenty-five-degree weather can turn into minus fifteen degrees at a moment's notice. And if you're deep in the mountains at the time, wearing nothing but short-sleeved clothing, you can die of hypothermia. A few people died just like that here not long ago."

Although I liked mountains, I was no serious hiker, so I didn't really need the advice. Unless maybe I wanted to commit suicide and even then there were better options.

Anyway, we paid him, thanked him, and then went to our hotel room where we ate the böreks, watched an episode of *Sunny in Philadelphia*, drank some beer, fucked—god knows where we managed to summon the energy for that—and then went to sleep.

The next day it was time to fly back home. I was pretty far from a patriot, but the longer I lived and the more I saw, the more I appreciated my home country.

DAY EIGHT
MONDAY

AFTER WE HAD breakfast in the morning, we fucked, had a shower, and then packed our bags. It was time to check out of the hotel. Since our plane left at seven in the evening, however, and it was only slightly after eleven in the morning, there was quite a bit of time left to kill, so we decided to wander around Ljubljana for a while.

We took a bus to the city center. Once there, we first went to take our backpacks to a locker in the train station, as we didn't want to carry them with us all day. But all the lockers were full. A guy there told us to take them to the lockers in the bus station instead, which we did.

It was the same dirty old understaffed central bus station, which we had visited a few days ago. It was packed full of people and had flies buzzing around, especially near the no doubt diarrhea-inducing sandwiches they sold there, its only "charming" aspect perhaps being the porn that was openly sold in one of its booths. And then of course there were the endless lines that never moved.

Although I hated lines, I guess what I *really* hated were the people that made up the lines. Not to mention the people that made those people. Didn't they consider that there might already be enough of them on this fucking planet? The selfish pricks! As far as I was concerned, wherever you saw endless lines or traffic jams or large crowds of people, you saw proof of overpopulation. Then again, for me even one person on this planet was a sign of overpopulation.

Anyway, after I stepped once again into Europe's worst bus station—go read some reviews online if you don't believe me—I couldn't help but gently wish that someone would bomb the place. That a meteor would land on it. That they nuked it from orbit. Hell, they might as well nuke the whole planet while we're at it.

After we had stood for a while in the line where the window said baggage, I noticed that there was also another area nearby that also said baggage, which looked more like a baggage storage area, and that one didn't have any lines. But when we went there the guy said you had to buy a ticket from the ticket office first, so we went back to standing in the same line again, which was now much longer.

Then, after a hundred trillion years had passed and the universe had suffered heat death, it was *finally* our turn. However, the lady told us that we had to pay at the window *afterwards* when we wanted to get our bags back. And so, we took the bags back to the baggage storage area again and got receipts which had to be paid for later in the ticket booth.

What a stupid, needlessly complex system, I thought. Also, since there was always an endless line in the bus station, what happened when you needed your bags in a hurry? I guess the stupid fucks who designed the system hadn't thought of that.

Afterwards, we went looking for something called Metelkova City Autonomous Cultural Centre, which had once been a military headquarters and which was now some strange alternative youth center with bars and clubs and graffiti and metal sculptures every-where.

When we arrived there, we saw that it was kind of pointless during the day since all the bars and clubs only opened during the evening, which is not to say that it wasn't equally pointless then, just in a differ-ent way. However, the place did somewhat have the look of a small post-apocalyptic town what with all the graffiti, run-down buildings, and strange metal sculptures everywhere, which was rather nice. It was good to see what the future would look like.

We then began walking towards the same park we had visited a few days ago, stopping on our way at a shop to buy some cold beer and ice cream because it was just so fucking hot outside.

In the shop, a Muslim woman was standing in the line in front of us with her customary three children and long black clothes, even though it was twenty-seven degrees outside. She was buying some maxi pads and as usual didn't say thank you or goodbye to the cashier when she left. I later saw her leave with her husband who was waiting further away. The man had a full grocery bag. I guess it was just too lowly for him to be buying maxi pads for his wife, so she had to do it alone.

We ate the ice creams whilst walking to the park. Once there, we sat down on a bench, opened our beers, and continued reading James Randi's *Encyclopedia*, discussing the entries along the way.

It never ceased to amaze me how much stupid shit people believed in—acupuncture and astrology and crystal healing and homeopathy and naturopathy and ley lines and dowsing and lizard people and black magic and voodoo and ghosts and spirits and angels and demons and mediums and chakras and feng shui and colon cleansing and gods and so on.

How come they didn't realize that all of these things were either misunderstandings or scams that were disproven a long time ago? Although all of us believed in stupid things, such as happiness or hope, some of us *really* crossed the threshold into pure fucking insanity. And by some, I mean most.

After the beers became too much for our bladders to handle, we got up and walked into the woods. I had downed my beers quite fast and felt a bit woozy. After we had emptied our bladders, we walked on deeper into the forest with an ulterior motive. Four cute dogs walked past us as we did.

Eventually, having found a good place between the shrubbery, I whipped it out, pulled Morrigan's pants down, and stuck it inside her. I fucked her until I was about to come and then pulled it out and came on some nearby leaves, the lucky bastards.

I STARTED PANICKING a little when we were cleaning up after sex since for some reason I thought that we only had twenty minutes to get back to the bus station, until Morrigan informed me that we actually had an hour and twenty minutes.

We thus thought of taking a little stroll through the nearby botanical garden, but when we walked to its front door, we saw that it was closed again, just like everything was in goddamn Slovenia.

Since there was a cafe nearby next to a pond, we decided to go there instead. We ordered some Laško beers and relaxed on the terrace, observing as a sparrow was trying to eat a sugar packet on the floor of the cafe.

Near us sat what appeared to be a family—a young girl typing on her smartphone, an old woman reading a paperback, and an old man reading a book on a tablet, occasionally dozing off. I wondered whether these people were so sick of each other that they didn't even talk anymore, or perhaps they had simply achieved such a level of social harmony that they didn't even need to speak anymore, everyone just doing their own thing, thinking their own thoughts. I liked to think that it was the latter, but the cynic in me suspected it was the former.

Then I suddenly noticed that it was only twenty minutes until the bus went to the airport. And this time I was right. So we quickly downed our beers and left. I snapped a quick "publicity photo" of Morrigan wearing a Dangerous Stories T-shirt by the nearby pond for my stupid little online "magazine"—by now defunct—and then we hurried to the bus station.

We took our bags and paid for the storage, arriving on the bus just in the nick of time. Once seated, we took a little nap as the bus drove towards the airport.

Fearing long lines, which was customary in airports after all, we were there two hours before our flight. However, there were no lines at all this time. In fact, we finished the check-in in about two minutes, which must have been a record. And so, we had a bunch of time to kill. Again.

Hungry as always, we went to a cafe and ordered two Brooklyn-style hot dogs and some beer. The food tasted like airport food usually tastes like—loveless.

And it was about as far from Brooklyn-style as North Korea was from a democracy.

While we were eating, I could hardly ignore the fact that some fucking kid was crying in the distance from the top of its—yes, *its*—lungs like it was getting raped. "What the goddamn fuck?" I said to Morrigan. "What kind of a dirtbag piece of shit parent lets their child scream like that in a public place?" The trip had awakened in me a newly renewed hatred against both children and so-called adults. The screaming went on for about fifteen more minutes and at one point I got so angry that I went looking for the mother.

When I located her, I wanted to yell from the top of my lungs: "LADY, SILENCE YOUR FUCKING KID!" But I feared that the airport security would then take me away and I'd miss the plane, so instead I just flashed her some bad looks and went back to my seat.

IN THE PLANE I ordered some beer and wine and a chicken bagel, using my otherwise useless frequent flyer points. The packaging on the chicken bagel said "artisanal" and "hand-made". What a crock of shit, I thought, as I bit into the mediocre-tasting bagel. Merely empty and meaningless marketing terms.

The adverts on the airplane monitors that constantly kept playing in the background in a feeble attempt at brainwashing you were likewise full of shit and completely untrue, making everything about the airline seem a hundred times better than it actually was. Alas, this was the norm in our deceitful little world. And the average person was simply too stupid to realize it, which is why the adverts worked.

For lack of anything better to do, I continued reading Bukowski, whilst sipping on my wine and beer, and Morrigan continued reading The Conspiracy Against the Human Race.

The flight, as usual, was boring and unpleasant. What made it even worse, however, was that when we began to land, I got a strong case of ear barotrauma, which stayed with me even while on the ground and neither yawning nor swallowing helped.

It was strange barely hearing anything around me, as though I was underwater. Strange and annoying. To add insult to injury, I had also somehow managed to pick up a flu, probably from some snotty little kid, and had to constantly blow my nose. Goddamn shit.

When we got to the Helsinki airport for the layover, I was dehydrated as hell since I had only drank beer and wine for a while now. However, all the shops were closed. One shop said, "We'll serve you 24/7," and yet it was closed. I clapped at their funny joke.

Eventually we managed to find one eating place that was still open where we could get some overpriced bottled water, after, of course, first having to stand in a line.

By that point, I was in a foul mood. I was tired. I'd

had enough of airports, airplanes, false advertising, bad food, overcrowded rooms, never-ending inconvenience, standing in lines, waiting, waiting, waiting, and, above all, human fucking beings—especially crowds of them.

As Bukowski said: "Wherever the crowd goes, run in the other direction. Because the crowd is always wrong." And nowhere was this more apparent than when it came to the giant overrated and overhyped nuisance known as traveling.

Eventually the connecting flight to Tallinn arrived and I would soon be home, where I could continue my usual more or less predictable and conveniently miserable existence.

To CONCLUDE WITH, making traveling "cheap" and "available for all" has largely ruined it because the only way to make it so is to make it appeal to the masses, who tend to be dumb as shit.

This in turn has ruined most travel destinations, for what tends to be missing from the colorful brochures is the commercialization and the souvenir shops and ticket machines and junk food stands and trash and confusion and noise and endless lines and crowds of low-IQ people taking pictures of god knows what, whilst their little parasites—aka children—run around screaming.

As such, I've often felt that a love for traveling is a

sign of stupidity. Which of course doesn't mean that you have to be stupid to travel, but rather that endlessly glorifying it and promoting it and talking about it with people who haven't asked and making it one of your primary character traits tends to be a sign of a stupid and shallow personality. Indeed, the urge to blow my brains out is rarely stronger than when standing next to such an asshole.

A saying amongst such people is that the world is a book and those who do not travel read only one page. Well, that's bullshit. Immanuel Kant never traveled. Yet there are plenty of cunts that travel extensively and do so only because everyone else is doing it and because they can then endlessly brag about it to others, making it seem much better than it actually is, as well as to post vain and narcissistic selfies online of their "adventures" abroad.

As though it was such an adventure to travel to the fucking Louvre and stand in a line for two hours just to get a glimpse at an overrated painting, or to go to a filthy overcrowded beach in Bali, or to get harassed by camel-fuckers in Egypt, or to catch E. coli in India, or to gamble away all your money in Las Vegas, or to visit superficial and materialistic Dubai in a country that in other respects is still stuck in the middle ages, or to simply spend your entire day by the pool at a fancy hotel that your (sugar) daddy paid for.

Because the truth is that there are no adventures

anymore in this world. Not since everything was bought and sold and turned into yet another product to be consumed by the masses. And folks, there is *nothing* less adventurous than a cheap experience that you can buy with money, just like everybody else.

As for me, the only way I could ever *enjoy* traveling would be if I could teleport from one place to the other, without having to suffer through the endless bullshit in-between. But *only* if a plague had first destroyed at least half the people on Earth. Or more.

And I know what you're thinking—that I just want the good without the bad. Well, guess what? *Everybody* does. Everybody wants the good and nobody wants the bad. Unfortunately there is very little of the good in this world and a whole lot of the bad. And the more people there are, the bigger is the competition between them to consume even the little good that the rich were kind enough to leave for the rest of us. And once we're all so busy consuming it, what do you think it is that *actually* remains?

Well, as the British tourists would say—fuck all, mate. Which is about as much as will remain of the planet once we humans are done with it.

THE END

ABOUT THE AUTHOR

Keijo Kangur is an author and occasional photographer from Estonia who has written poetry, film and video game reviews, historical and philosophical articles, short stories, and a novel. He writes in both Estonian and English.

Coming from a working-class background, he has worked as a telemarketer, in construction, at a warehouse, at a pizza parlor, as a postal sorter, at call centers, as a data entry clerk, for an airline, and as an anti-money laundering investigator.

Although he has never been to college, he has spent years studying philosophy, science, and literature. From his studies and life experience, he has developed views which may be compared to those most famously expressed by Rust Cohle in the TV series True Detective. Above all, he considers himself an antinatalist.

His favorite fiction tends to be the kind that is based on the author's own life and focuses on the darker side of existence. His own works likewise draw strongly from his real-life experiences and revolve around the darker aspects of being.

Despite all this, he *does* possess a sense of humor and tries not to take himself too seriously all the time.

Giant Meteor
2020
JUST END IT ALREADY

Please consider leaving a short review on Amazon or Goodreads.

Thank you.

Printed in Great Britain
by Amazon